MARK OF A DEMON

Cover Illustration: Evangelos Dimou
www.iamevandimu.com
Editing-Correction: Despoina Kemeridou, Evangelos Dimou
Pagination: Evangelos Dimou

ISBN: 978-618-85153-0-7

© 2020 SELF-PUBLISHING "KEMERIDOU"
DESPOINA KEMERIDOU
website: www.kemeridou.com
email: books@kemeridou.com

A PARANORMAL ROMANCE SHORT STORY

MARK OF A DEMON

by Despoina Kemeridou

www.kemeridou.com
2020

Contents

CHAPTER 1

A Life for A Life

From the day I opened my eyes in this world, my fate had already been sealed. I was never given the opportunity to choose what I wanted. A higher power determined everything, and I searched in vain for a way to change it.

When I was born, the midwives insisted that I wouldn't survive the night and my poor mother inquired nonstop about my health. She kept praying to some god to give me strength to live. Unsuccessfully though, because my condition worsened with every passing second.

"Your child's heart is weak."

"She might not live to see the morning sun."

"There is nothing else we can do."

"Not even a miracle can save the poor child."

When the sun set, a midwife took me to my mother's room, explaining that it would be better to spend my last moments with her. My father died not two months before my birth, so it was her sister who was now by her side – the only person she trusted. The scent of lavender was everywhere inside the bedroom. Seemed like my aunt had brought those flowers as a gift to my mother. It was the first and last time I experienced that smell.

My aunt sighed. "She couldn't stand the loss of her father and now she's yearning to meet him."

My mother cried as she hugged me tightly. "I'll do it, Sara. The gods don't seem to hear my prayers today. I'll do it, even if I'm going to be punished. I only wish for my child to live. I can't stand to lose her, too!" she said sobbing.

"Don't be stupid, Lorelei! Demons are evil creatures."

"I don't care."

Then, she put me in my bed. She crossed her hands together as if she was praying and spoke in another language, one I couldn't understand.

Hear me, Spirits of the Night
Demons of Darkness
and Fallen Angels.
My child can't live anymore
and time back will not go.
I heard she won't survive the night
and no god to my prayers will answer.
I urge you to come forth.
Whoever is capable,
riches many will receive
and all that they will ask for.
Even my life I would give,
if my child was to be saved.

A bright, black sphere appeared in front of her, and a human figure came out of it; a tall, young man with red eyes, like an ever-burning hellfire, and black hair like a moonless night. His clothes were strange, for all around him black flames danced. It was as if he had come from another world. He didn't speak, only looked at my mother with his cold gaze.

She was baffled, while my aunt backed off at the sight. They knew that the creature that responded to the prayer wasn't human; not a god and not an angel either.

"Who… are you?" my mother stammered.

"I am Naberius, one of Hell's most powerful demons. The price for what you're asking of me is great," he said with his deep and hoarse voice.

"I'll give you anything you want!" my mother exclaimed in desperation.

"To save a life, you must sacrifice another. I will give you one day to decide. Do not worry, your child will survive the night."

Exactly as he appeared out of nowhere, he now disappeared into the darkness of the night. My mother was so terrified she almost fainted.

"I'll give my life…" she mumbled.

"Don't do it, Lorelei! Let the child die. You can see it too; she's not meant to live. You can't change her fate."

"It's my child, Sara. I won't leave it to fate's mercy," she said, griping onto the armchair next to her.

"You're so stubborn, just like when you were younger. When will you finally learn your lesson?"

"I lost my husband. If I lose my child too, that's it. I'm ruined. Why don't you understand?"

"You are the one who doesn't understand. The demons won't feel sorry for you. They will stab you in the back when you least expect it. They won't hesitate to deceive you. They will detach your soul from your body, just to let it burn forever in Hell. The baby will live, but at some point, the demon's powers will run out. Her life will be temporary and thus will belong to him. Is this what you want? Is this the right thing?"

"I have already made up my mind. Nothing will stop me now – not even you."

*

The night passed quickly and the next day arrived. The *doomsday*, as my aunt called it. My mother took a hot bath, brushed her hair, and wore her most beautiful dress. Sara silently witnessed her last moments, regretting how she failed to change her mind. In her thoughts, she almost hated me.

With all the preparations, the light of day disappeared and the moon was now up high in the sky, while the stars kept it company. As promised, the demon finally appeared at the same place he was first called, his gaze fiercer than before.

"Have you made your decision?"

She looked over at me with eyes wet and full of worry. "Yes. I know very well what it is you want."

"What do I want, then?"

"My life, in exchange for my daughter's."

The corner of his lips curled upward in a sarcastic smirk. "Your life, her life, for all I care. One life for another."

"Nothing is keeping me in this world anymore. Save my child and do what you want with me," she said, clenching her fists.

A spark lit in the demon's red eyes. His impatience couldn't be hidden. Still, his gaze remained cold. "I'll only give you a warning. Your child won't live for many years. Maybe until her twenties, who knows? As long as my power allows. Sharing a heart with a human gradually drains a demon's powers."

"It's enough, it doesn't matter." She turned to my aunt and looked at her, her eyes filled with sorrow. "Sara, you were the best sister I could ever ask for. You've always been by my side. Even in my worst moments, you were always there. You always laughed with every little nonsense I said and did. I'm trusting my daughter to you now. If it's you, I know she'll be in good hands. She will be the child you were never able to have. And if I'm selfish, I hope one day, you will be able to forgive me."

It was the first time Sara wept. She hugged my mother for one last time, as she embraced me and then left me into my aunt's hands. She approached the demon without looking back and disappeared along with him.

Chapter 2

A New Beginning

I haven't seen my mother since then. She disappeared like a shooting star, one that fades before you can even get a glimpse of it. Aunt Sara started taking care of me. She collected all the valuable belongings we had in the mansion and dragged me along on horses and carriages. She kept saying it was cursed. She found a small house in a quiet village and decided it would be better there.

Ten years after my birth, I attended school. Since I had a mark high on my chest from birth, my aunt always forced me to wear clothes that hid it. She said it was evil and it would bring me bad luck if someone saw it. I, on the other hand, thought it was beautiful.

It looked like a heather, from which I got my name. My aunt liked to call me Eri.

"Sara, I don't like school. I don't want to go there anymore," I complained.

"Eri, I thought we talked about this."

"No-one wants to be my friend because of my green eyes!"

"Don't mind them, my dear. They are just jealous. Do you know how many of them would like to have eyes like yours?" she responded.

I knew that wasn't exactly the case. I had a special ability; from the day I was born, besides the real world, I could see creatures that weren't visible to the human eye. And somewhere, deep inside them, the children in the school knew. They called me a witch, an elf, a demon... I didn't know what I was, nor did I want to know either.

One morning, I heard my aunt talking to a neighbor.

"What do you mean, Sara?"

"Exactly what you heard. I'm almost broke and I don't want Eri to stop going to school. I relied too much on my sister's property, but I don't have a man nor a job."

"You have to get married. Time won't wait for you. That poor guy, Peter, has been in love with you for so many years. He can help you financially, both you and your little girl."

"I don't know… I'm getting old. He wouldn't look at me now. I'll just find a job. There will surely be someone who needs a healer."

"I'll talk to everyone I know, but I don't think Peter minds your wrinkles."

"Come on, Brianna, leave now. We'll wake the kid up. She doesn't have school today."

Once I tiptoed out of the room, I found my aunt, with arms crossed, standing at the bottom of the stairs.

"Did Brianna's loud voice wake you up again?"

I didn't want to tell her I heard everything, so I lied. "No, I just got up," I answered, avoiding her gaze.

If there was something in this world, I wasn't good at, it was lying. To make matters worse, I couldn't lie to Sara.

To my surprise, she smiled and went to the kitchen to prepare breakfast. She didn't eat. Instead, I watched her take a large, dusty bag out of the storeroom, to the left side of the kitchen. She cleaned it and opened it carefully. Inside, there were all kinds of bottles, notes, and dried plants.

"Sara? Are you a witch?"

After studying the amusement on my face and listening intently to my question, she laughed. "No, my child. I'm a healer. I mean, I was once."

"And why did you stop?" I insisted, tilting my head to the side.

"When I lost my husband, I found no pleasure in what I was doing and, one day, I just stopped."

"Do you make magic potions, too?"

She laughed again. "I make magic potions, too, yes," she said with a sly look.

I smiled broadly at her.

*

The days passed and my aunt began to visit many homes as a healer. I heard she was excellent at her job. One day, someone asked her to prepare medicine for his feet, which hurt a lot.

She wore a dress that wasn't torn or had any patches, and she brushed her blonde hair, that had begun to turn white. She held her heavy bag in one hand and me in the other. Since it wasn't a school day, I had to go with her, as she was afraid to leave me alone at home. After a long walk, we finally arrived. My aunt knocked on the door twice. When she saw the man who opened it, she turned red.

"Peter!" she exclaimed, a derisive edge to her voice.

"You weren't expecting to see me here, were you? Come on in!"

Peter was a kind-hearted man. His hair was white and he had a bald spot on the back of his head, although he wasn't much older than Sara. In the past, he had proposed to her, but my aunt rejected him.

"Well, Peter, what is your problem?" she said, as he seemed to be perfectly fine.

"It's not me. My nephew, Finn. For days now, he's been unable to walk properly because his feet are hurting. Come and see for yourself."

Sara followed him, while I stayed in the dining room eating the biscuits Peter offered me. I couldn't stay still. I grabbed as many biscuits as my hands could hold and walked around the house. There were all kind of paintings hanging on the walls. *How much did he pay for all these pieces?* I couldn't believe my eyes. Before I realized it, I had eaten all of the biscuits.

Their voices disrupted my excitement. They finally came out of that room. I could hear everything, even though they were trying to speak quietly.

"Don't worry, Peter. You only have to give him this medicine once a day and put this ointment on his feet. After a while, he will be able to walk normally again."

"I don't know how to thank you."

"There's no need."

"Listen, Sara. I know I've said it in the past, but nothing has changed. My proposal is still valid. My home is huge and I have no-one else to share it with. Come and stay with me and bring your niece, too. I'll send her to a better school, if she wants to."

Silence prevailed for a while, enough to feel awkward.

My aunt finally replied, "Peter... I..." she stammered and then took a deep breath. "It will be my pleasure to become your wife. Besides, I think a male presence is necessary for Eri."

I think Peter hugged her from his joy. When they came back, my aunt was blushing again and Peter was smiling.

"Eri! You ate all the biscuits?"

"I'm sorry..."

She sighed. "What am I going to do with this kid?"

Peter laughed. Sara took a deep breath and looked straight at me. I thought she was going to scold me.

"Would you like it, if we came to live in this house?"

My eyes widened and a large smile appeared on my face. "I would love to! It's bigger and it's got all those weird paintings. Can we really move in here?"

I saw her eyes full of relief as she turned her gaze to Peter. "Seems like Eri really likes your house. You can come whenever you wish to help us with the moving."

"You will be a great company for me and Finn," he said and touched my shoulder.

After that, we headed home.

The very next day, Peter came to help us pack our things. He loaded all of them in a carriage and we left from that embarrassing little house once and for all.

His house had two floors and was very spacious, with many rooms and a beautiful dining area. I let the grown-ups put the things we brought in order and took a look around the second floor. It wasn't anything special and the decoration was minimal in contrast to the first floor. This house was much better than our previous one. When I finished my exploration, I went to my new room and fell asleep.

*

The days were going by swiftly in our new home. My aunt and Peter decided to live together, but not to marry, at least for now. Every day I saw them, they became happier and happier.

Peter's nephew, Finn, was cured and started walking again normally. Even though he lived with us, he often preferred to ride his horse in the woods or to the city. Every time he came back, he brought biscuits and chocolates, to which my aunt scolded him. Later, I learned that his parents had died and he'd been staying with Peter ever since then. He was three years older than me.

I loved reading. Apart from the exquisite paintings, Uncle Peter also collected all kinds of books in his bookcase. I used to read a lot. Most of them seemed to refer to otherworldly beings like angels and demons. We were taught about them from a young age, but I always wanted to know more. They were a part of our culture. Since I kept seeing those weird creatures around me, I was extremely interested in that kind of books.

By the years, I learned to act as if they didn't exist, so that I could look like a normal girl. Well, I knew I wasn't, but I wanted to be. At least for once, I prayed that mark would disappear along with those creatures. I was lucky they never talked to me. They just looked at me with their eerie gazes and made my whole body shiver. I came to the conclusion they were lost souls, that, for some reason, haven't been accepted neither in heaven, nor in Hell.

According to my uncle's books, angels and demons were once human. When they died, their souls went to either Heaven or Hell, depending on their past actions. Not all of them could become angels or demons. The souls who were full of regrets, guilt, or they had committed serious crimes during their human lives, would forever roam in the world of the living, never able to leave or find eternal rest.

Heaven and Hell each had their own King. They were in charge of the course of angels and demons respectively. They were also responsible for their awarding and punishing. Not all people believed in the existence of these two worlds and their beings, but I didn't have a choice. Some also claimed they were just myths, created to terrify the mischievous children.

It seemed like people of both genders with green eyes and red hair have always been stigmatized. I was lucky that my aunt was a respected healer in our village, so the teasing only happened at school.

CHAPTER 3

Guardian Demon

One day, when I came back from school, I found Sara and Peter in the dining room, talking.

"I'm back..." I said with a trace of dissatisfaction in my voice.

"Eri! Did something happen, my child?" my aunt asked, when she saw my obvious distaste.

"Today the children in school said I was cursed, and nobody would approach me."

Sara turned to Peter for a moment and he nodded at her.

"Heather, what would you say about going to another school?"

"I would love to, Uncle Peter, but the only school I can attend needs money, and only a few children from this village are accepted."

"If you want to, we can send an application and see what happens."

"Thank you, Uncle Peter! I truly want to."

I embraced both of them and ran into my room full of excitement. It wasn't easy to believe that there was even a small chance of changing schools. It gave me hope that I wouldn't have to suffer for the next seven years of my life.

After we sent the application, the days dragged on, so much so that I found myself checking the mailbox every hour. With each day that passed, my hope transformed into fear, until one day, the letter arrived. My fingers danced across the back to open it, nearly destroying its contents. I scanned every word thoroughly, eyes wide, and then ran into the house to announce, "I got accepted!"

Aunt Sara jumped up and down and Peter gently patted my shoulder.

"Do your homework and listen to your teachers," he told me.

"Peter and I have already got you some new dresses to wear to your new school. We hope you like them."

Entering my room, I looked at the dresses one by one. They were much more gorgeous than those I've been wearing until now. I was overjoyed.

My school was now in the opposite direction of the previous one and I went along with Finn frequently. From the very first day, I became good friends with Christie, a petite girl my age who loved singing. She approached me first. In contrast to the others that hated my red hair and green eyes, she said she loved them very much.

The usual problems had already begun with my other schoolmates. The color of my eyes was evil, according to their words, and I was a witch that sold her soul to the devil, so I had to be hanged or better, burned. To tell the truth, things weren't as bad as before. At least now I had Christie, who didn't care at all about what the others were saying.

Every month, my teachers reported to Sara and Peter on my progress. Not once did they say anything negative, and that made them very proud of me. Over time, I also learned to ignore my classmates' insults. I knew I was different and I had already accepted it. I always acted as if I couldn't hear them. I didn't want to allow their words to hurt me. So, little by little, teasing and mockery seemed to cease.

*

After four years at the same school, the boredom sunk in. Finn began to help Uncle Peter in the stable, since he had nothing better to do. Although it wasn't necessary, every morning he took me to school on the horse.

"For protection," he kept saying as an excuse.

I wasn't *that* stupid. I found out he liked me, but I didn't feel anything for him. There were many times he tried to hold my hand as I was dismounting the horse. Some other times, I caught him awkwardly smiling at me. Occasionally, he would also flirt with stupid quotes like 'Would you like to ride until we reach our magical kingdom?' or 'Do you think we will stay here forever? Because I wouldn't mind spending forever with you.' Yes. I hated it and most of those times, I didn't answer.

They never stopped teasing me at school, but they gradually did it less and less. I almost started to believe my suffering would end from time to time. Things, however, changed one of the days that Christie got sick and had to stay at home.

As always, in our free time, I decided to go and read a book at my favorite spot; a wooden bench, away from the noise of the other kids. Nobody ever came to that place, as it was hidden by the shadow of a weeping willow tree and it was quite far from the main yard. I normally sat there with Christie and we talked about classes and boys.

All of a sudden, Marcie, along with Avery and Nerissa, approached me with their sneaky smiles and stood in front of me, studying me with their scary eyes.

"Hello witch!" said Avery with a tone of irony in her annoyingly high-pitched voice.

"Where is your faithful pet today?" Marcie added.

"I hope you didn't sacrifice her in one of your rituals!" continued Nerissa.

Turning her gaze at the book I was holding, Marcie snatched it away from me and threw it on the ground. Nerissa held out a pocket knife, that she had probably stolen from her house and proceeded to tear my book apart. Instinctively, I approached her and tried to stop her. After all, it was my favorite book.

Everything happened so quickly, that I never understood how her knife ripped off my dress, on the spot where my birthmark was. She probably didn't intend to, but she cut my skin as well, because hot blood started running from the wound. I had to hold the torn dress in place so that my secret wouldn't be revealed. For that reason, I couldn't react when they pushed me and started kicking me. It hurt so much, but I was frozen and desperately tried to hold back my tears. No-one was there to help me.

Around me, the strange creatures were looking at me from afar, but they suddenly began to back away, terrified. It was the first time I saw them that afraid. Then, I realized; it was another creature that looked familiar, but I couldn't remember where I've seen it before. He had black hair, just like the darkest night and red eyes, as if a fire was burning inside of them. On his back he had two black wings.

The girls couldn't see him. His ice-cold gaze met my eyes for a moment, then turned to the three girls. Raising his right hand, he sent all three of them flying in the air. They landed farther away from me. They looked at each other with eyes wide open and, without saying another word, they ran away crying and screaming. If I wasn't wounded, I would have laughed extremely hard. But I was in a lot of excruciating pain and worried about the blood that didn't seem to stop. The creature approached me and fell on his knees.

"I should have come earlier. Are you all right?" he said, his hoarse voice echoing everywhere.

I nodded, still holding my bloodied dress. My heart was pounding fast. I couldn't understand if it was because of him, or because I was at the verge of death. He touched my wound. His hand felt surprisingly warmer than my skin, making my heart skip another beat.

I didn't feel any more pain, nor did I see any blood flowing. Looking at the spot where the wound once was, I realized it was no longer there. I heard the bell signifying the end of my break.

"Everyone will wonder what happened, if they see me in this mess," I said worried.

His fiery eyes looked straight at me. "I can fix your dress, but I will leave those bruises and scratches on your face and hands. It's better if you have proof of what they did to you."

"They'll get punished."

"Isn't that the right thing?"

He is right. They should be punished. I never did anything to them, so why is it that they were allowed to mistreat me like that and destroy my favorite book?

I smiled. "I like you." His eyes widened with surprise. "You're a demon, aren't you?"

A faint smile appeared on his face. "The feathers give it away, eh?" He raised his hand and fixed my torn dress. "Better head straight to the Principal."

"Thank you for helping me," I said and hurried back inside.

Like he advised me, I didn't go to the classroom first. Many students were afraid of the Principal, but I always thought she was quite likable. She was the only female Principal in our area. It was extremely rare to see a woman in that position.

"What happened, Miss Heather? Who did this to you?" she said worried when she saw my bruised body and my messed-up hair.

"Marcie, Nerissa and Avery attacked me during our break. Look what they did to my book," I said and showed her the book they had ripped apart.

Mrs. Charlotte was speechless and her face turned pale. "This could only be done with a knife. Why would three of my students have a knife in their possession?"

The Principal was a gentle, but very strict woman. I knew she liked me, because I was quiet and never caused any problems. She wouldn't believe those girls, even if they told her exactly what happened.

"It was a pocket knife."

She sighed heavily and gave me permission to leave. I got back to my classroom, ignoring everyone's stare, took my books and went back home by foot. I followed a path from which no-one would see me. I didn't want to cause any commotion.

"I'm back," I said when I got in.

"Eri? What are you doing here so early?" my aunt replied from the kitchen.

As I got closer, she ran to me. "What happened to you?" she exclaimed and checked up on my bruises.

"I was attacked by some girls from my class. It's nothing, Sara, honestly. I didn't let them see the mark."

"What about the blood? Who got hit?"

Indeed, there were some drops of blood on the destroyed book I was holding. I had to get rid of that before Sara could see it, but I forgot. "Me. I got hurt, when they tore my dress, but then, a demon came and saved me. He healed my wound and replaced my dress," I replied, as my aunt knew about my special ability.

Her face turned pale, but she didn't say anything. She prepared the bath for me and took care of the bruises from the beating. Then, she gave me some hot jasmine tea, which I genuinely liked. After I calmed down a bit, I went to sleep.

The next day, I didn't go to school. My aunt advised me to stay home, thinking I would be safer that way. Peter and Finn wanted to pamper me, because they were worried about what happened, but Sara was scolding them and telling them I would be spoiled. Christie also came to visit me after school.

"I'm telling you, Heather, everyone is talking about it. Marcie, Nerissa and Avery are changing schools. There are rumors that they attacked you and they feel bad about it."

"Look, I'm all good, Christie. Nothing bad happened. If they want to go, fine. I never liked them anyway."

"Oh, if only I hadn't gotten sick! You are my only friend. I don't want you to get hurt."

We talked for a while before saying goodbye, as the sun had almost set.

*

I wasn't proud of how lightly I slept. My aunt's voice woke me up. It looked like she was arguing with someone. The sound was coming from the kitchen. I knew that Sara and Peter didn't fight often, nor would they act like little children in the middle of the night. As I grew closer, their words became clear.

"I didn't want it, Sara. She is the one who called me. I don't know how, but she did. I couldn't bear to see her suffer," a familiar, hoarse voice said.

"I told you, Naberius. She must never know who you are. I made you promise me something fourteen years ago. Don't you dare break that promise. You will not tell her. She doesn't have to know."

"I'll protect her from afar, as much as I can. I won't approach her anymore. However, one day I will return – wait for me. I will return to take back what's mine –"

Trying to get closer, I stumbled upon a chair and made a loud noise. My aunt came to me first. "Eri! What are you doing here?"

"Uhm, you know, I –"

Behind her, there was a creature with black wings. Looking at him closely, I came to realize he was the demon who saved me at school. It was hard to forget those eyes. Before I could say another word, he ran up to me and put his hand on my head. My eyes opened wide and my heart skipped a beat from his sudden move. A sudden feeling of dizziness came over me and I felt like I was losing consciousness. Someone held me in their arms. This is the last thing I remember before falling into a deep sleep and forgetting all I have seen that night.

CHAPTER 4

First Kiss

The next morning, I was pretty sure I had an extremely important dream, but I couldn't remember it and finally gave up trying. I saw Sara looking at me suspiciously, but I decided not to pay any attention.

I went to school as normal. Marcie, Avery, and Nerissa would never come back here again. My other classmates seemed terrified, but they didn't stop saying such things to me as 'witch', 'you should burn at the stake', 'demonic woman' and other such names.

As long as they didn't touch me, I didn't care. As long as they didn't see my mark, I didn't mind. They would hang me at the village square and torture me until the blood had dried up from my veins. To tell you the truth, only the thought of it sent an icy shiver down my spine. However, for the time being, I was safe at the school.

That day, Christie and I went to the wooden bench and sat there together. At least now, I wouldn't be bothered by anyone.

"Have you noticed how handsome Finn is? You are so lucky you get to see him and be with him every day."

"As far as I'm concerned, he mostly gets on my nerves."

"He always seems so calm. How is that possible?" she scratched her head.

"A few days ago, I was reading a book by the fireplace. He knew Sara and Peter weren't around, so he came and sat beside me. I didn't mind at first, but he started talking to me, and you know it annoys me when others talk while I'm reading. Then, he came closer and proceeded to hug me."

"I'm sure he just sees you as a little sister. He's already overprotective with you."

I scoffed. "Christie, I think that's enough of Finn today. I'm really not in the mood to talk about him."

"Hmph!" she complained.

Turning my gaze to the willow's branch, I saw the familiar silhouette of the demon standing there. He was looking straight at me, as if he was trying to keep me safe, so no harm would come my way. When he realized I caught him, he opened his lips – maybe he was trying to say something – but he closed them again and chose only to smile. I blushed as my heart started pounding fast. Christie gave me a suspicious look, but the significant bell sound interrupted all of her thoughts. We silently went back to the classroom.

*

At the entrance to the courtyard of the school, Finn was waiting for me on his horse. He rarely came to get me, so I was used to going home with Christie. I climbed on the horse and thanked him for coming.

"After what happened, I'm thinking of coming every day."

"Come on, Finn. Really, you don't have to."

"But how did you get back home in such a mess? Weren't you afraid?"

"I took the road that leads to the river."

"I should have been there."

"Don't worry about me. You should stay and help Uncle Peter. He needs you."

We stopped at the stable, but I didn't see Peter anywhere. I started feeling uncomfortable.

"Why did we come here?" I asked him as soon as he got off his horse.

"Come down and I'll tell you," he said calmly.

Finally, I got off too, without speaking. He grabbed my hand and led me to the warehouse, where we kept the necessaries for the horses.

"Finn, we have to go home. I have homework to do and I don't want Sara to worry."

"She knows I came here to get you."

"Fine, but you still haven't told me why you brought me here."

"Heather, the truth is, I can't get you off my mind lately. I am a bit older than you and you always treat me like a brother, but I see you in a different way. I don't know what else to do for you to understand it. I love you."

Everything I was afraid to hear, I finally heard. I liked him, but I couldn't see him in a romantic way.

"I love you too, Finn, but I will never be able to be your lover," I said after a few minutes of silence.

"You won't know, if you don't try."

Before I could react, he approached my face and pressed his lips against mine. I didn't feel a single thing from that kiss. It wasn't because of the way he kissed me. It was because I didn't feel anything for him. I pushed him impulsively, so hard that he fell down. Be it Peter's nephew or not, he didn't have the right to deprive me of my first kiss. Furious, I left running, following the road to the house. When I went inside, I didn't say a thing. I only looked at my aunt with teary eyes and locked myself in my room.

Outside, it started raining. I sat by the window waiting for Finn to return. The time was passing by and I gradually started feeling bored. When I was about to fall asleep, I saw him come into the yard, soaked to the bone. *Sara will surely scold him now!* I walked out of the room and stood on top of the stairs. He looked at me with a hurt gaze and turned his head to the living room, where my aunt sat, ignoring me.

"Finn! What happened to you?" she exclaimed, worried.

"Leave me alone, Sara. I'm not in the mood to hear your complaints right now. I was outside and I didn't manage to get back in time," he replied abruptly and walked swiftly to the bathroom.

"This kid is going to get in trouble one day," she murmured.

Sara saw me standing there. I acted like I was just looking around and returned to my room. It didn't take long for her to knock on the door.

"Eri, we need to talk."

Now I'm in trouble. I opened the door hesitantly.

She walked in and sat on the edge of my bed. "Tell me, my child. Didn't Finn come to school to get you today?"

"He did."

"And why didn't you come back together?"

"Sara…"

"I knew it! Something happened between you two, didn't it?"

I blushed and lowered my head.

"Look, you have to talk to me. I want to know what happened."

"You see… Finn took me to the stable instead of home. He told me he loved me and he kissed me."

"He kissed you? On the lips?"

My aunt was furious. Her cheeks had turned red from anger. She was almost ready to go teach him a lesson or two, but she tried to remain calm.

"Yes, on the lips."

"What did you do?"

"Nothing. I don't love Finn. He's like a brother to me and nothing more."

"Nothing else happened, then? Anything serious?"

"No, don't worry. But now he's mad at me and he won't talk to me ever again," I said distressed.

"His anger will go away and you will be friends again, just like the old times. Give him a little time."

"I hope so. We were… friends."

It was already dark outside. Sara kissed me goodnight and closed the door behind her.

All night, I kept thinking about what a stupid thing Finn had done this time. What if that kiss continued and I wasn't able to react? What would have happened then? Sara and Peter would insist on us marrying and my whole life would be ruined. I had to stay away for a while. But how would I be able to do that, while living in the same house? Searching for a solution to my problem, I didn't get any sleep that night.

Fortunately, the next morning I didn't have school. I didn't want to enter the classroom with those red eyes and dark circles. I went to the kitchen to eat. It seemed that nobody was up yet. I started preparing bread with cheese for breakfast. Sara used to make more tasty meals, but I was feeling very tired at that moment to do anything else.

After some time passed, I heard footsteps approaching. I turned my head only to see Finn standing behind me. Perfect. Exactly what I needed to start off my day.

"Good morning," he said first.

"Good morning," I replied.

He sat on one of the kitchen's chairs. "Heather… Forget about what happened. I was a fool and I wasn't thinking straight. I put you in a difficult situation and made things awkward for us. Forgive me and let us be friends again, just like we were before. I can't bear not being able to talk to you."

Looking at him closely, his eyes seemed as red as mine. I had to forgive him and move on. "I forgot everything already, Finn. That kiss meant nothing to me. All good?"

"All good," he exclaimed and a somewhat fake smile appeared on his face.

It didn't take long for Peter and Sara to wake up. When they saw us telling jokes and laughing like little kids, they nodded at each other and decided to sit in the living room, so that they wouldn't bother us.

We remained in the kitchen almost all day. I had exhausted every single detail for my school life and my classmates. I also told him about Christie, how admirable and sweet she was. Time went by before we knew it. It was dark outside and we were still there. When we realized it, we laughed it off and returned to our rooms.

I was glad that Finn wasn't mad at me. I hadn't done anything wrong, I just hurt his feelings. However, I didn't seem to stop feeling uncomfortable around him and I thought I'd never manage to get over it.

While I was lost in my thoughts, I remembered that creature that protected me. All my life, I knew angels were the ones who were supposed to protect us. But... a demon? *Why would he protect me? So many people in this world need help and he chose me? Me?* I giggled, as I remembered how those girls were tossed in the air. It's not something I would do, even if I had the power to. Obviously, I would just sit there until I fainted from the pain, or until they left me alone. If I had a choice, I'd get up and run away. I was a coward, but I was weak, too. I was able to see those weird creatures, but I couldn't communicate with them. One time, in fact, I saw one so terrifying, I had to take another route home.

All that thinking made me sleepy. I slept like a log that night. When I woke up, I realized I overslept and had to run to arrive at school in time. Finn later told me he tried waking me up, but I wasn't listening, so he left a bit earlier.

CHAPTER 5

Nabe

Three years passed. That demon kept visiting me at school. He always stood by the weeping willow tree. It seemed as if he liked it. I never really thought that demons had the ability to like anything, let alone love. I once tried to talk to him, but he quickly disappeared from my sight. *Maybe he is shy? Are demons shy?* After that day, he didn't visit me again. I was sure he was hiding somewhere else, further away from me, tirelessly waiting for me to return home safely.

It was winter and all the trees had been deprived of their precious leaves. The sky was always cloudy and the snow was falling endlessly. Outside, everything was painted white. Fortunately, we had a fireplace at home. Every night, all of us used to sit in the living room, near the fire and talk for hours. I didn't have school because of the bad weather, since you could barely go out and walk on those slippery, icy roads.

One of those days, Finn went to the stable to check on the horses. He was taking far too long to return, making me more and more worried as time passed. I put on the warmest clothes I could find in my wardrobe and followed the path to the stable. I didn't want to bother Sara, because Peter was sick with fever and she was taking care of him with medicine and herbs. After finally getting there, I tried calling Finn many times, but nobody answered. It didn't seem like he was there anymore.

All of a sudden, the weather worsened. Heavy gusts came in whipping my hair around, as the snow cascaded over me. I could hardly walk. I tried to leave, but the wind wouldn't let me. I couldn't get in the warehouse either, because the snow had piled up in front of the door, sealing it. I was struggling in vain. A few moments later, I quit trying and lost my senses.

The cold snow was covering me, freezing every inch of my body. Then, a familiar face came to my mind and a name spontaneously escaped my pale, almost purple lips, "Naberius."

One second later, I stopped feeling cold and the snow melted from my body. I slowly regained consciousness and opened my eyes. It was him. He came. I don't know how, but I knew his name and called out to him.

"Heather! Are you okay?" he asked, his eyes wide of worry.

At that moment, I wondered if demons could be worried. "I'm fine or, at least, that's what I believe. I'm not dead, am I?" I said, still feeling a bit weak.

He smiled at me and held me tightly in his arms. "When you called me and I saw you like that, I was so scared. I can cure your wounds, but I can't bring you back to life. Now, tell me honestly, how did you know my name?"

"I don't know. I just thought of you and it came to me."

"I should have stayed closer to you. Listen, if you ever need me again, I will come by your side."

He touched my hand and, for some strange reason, I felt my chest tighten. I expected his hands to be cold due to the freezing temperature. To my surprise, they were warmer than most humans'.

I felt like an invisible force was pushing me to embrace him. I didn't dare to, even though I was craving for his touch. It's not that I was afraid, but he was still a demon. I only managed to hold his hand.

Before I knew it, we had already arrived home. I was surprised, but I thanked him. I would never get used to his supernatural powers.

"I don't know what would have happened, if you hadn't come. Why are you protecting me?"

"I care about you, Heather. The truth is that I had made a promise to Sara, never to appear in front of you again, but I can't bear to see you suffer. I broke that promise so many times already and I would break it a thousand more for you. You could have died today; do you know that?"

"But why me? Why did you choose me?"

"You don't need to know. Not yet."

He approached me and did what I've been hesitating to do. His embrace was warm, just like a summer day during the cold winter. I didn't know a thing about him, but everything just felt so familiar, as if I knew him from when I was still a baby. As if he was my destiny.

When he was about to leave, I said goodbye, waving at him as I entered the house. I ran directly to the fireplace. Finn was constantly asking me if I was alright and he apologized for being late. Seemed like he took another route home. It didn't take long for me to fall asleep, listening to the sound of the fire burning the woods, and the wind blowing furiously on the windows of the house.

"Eri! Eri!"

I heard my aunt's voice and I jolted, getting up from the couch, as if someone had stung me.

"What? What happened?"

"You slept here last night."

"Oh, Sara, I was so tired that I fell asleep before I even knew it."

"It's all right, my child. Come on, I prepared breakfast for you."

I followed her to the kitchen. It seemed like the others had already eaten, as mine was the only dish left on the table.

"Are Peter and Finn not here?"

"No. They left before you woke up. The sun is up and shining and the snow started melting. They said they'd check for any damages at the stable and be back for lunch."

As I was eating, I remembered what happened yesterday. My aunt started glancing suspiciously at me. It was probably written all over my face that something was going on.

"What's wrong, Eri? You know you can't hide anything from me."

"I know, Sara. I won't lie to you. Yesterday, at the stable, I almost died. I fainted after the snow covered me and called Naberius for help. You know him too, don't you?"

Sara turned pale. "How do you know his name? I told him to stay away from you."

"I didn't know it. I needed him and his name just popped up in my mind. I don't want to stay away from him. He may be a demon but he is the one who saved me back then, at the school. He's kind."

"I see a dangerous spark in your eyes, Eri. It's better to forget about it. Where did you see a human and a demon together? Tell me."

"You don't understand. He doesn't mean any harm."

"He's going to hurt you."

"But Sara –"

"This conversation is over. I have nothing else to say to you. Go to your room and do your homework. Tomorrow you'll be able to go to school again."

I didn't dare utter another word. The conversation was, indeed, over. I went to my room in a hurry and slammed the door behind me.

One day, I'm going to be punished for this…

"Naberius," I whispered.

He appeared through a black sphere and looked at me surprised. I advised him to stay quiet and he obeyed.

"I wanted to see you," I finally told him and he smiled.

"That's why you called me?"

"It's one of the reasons, yes. Listen, Naberius, or rather, Nabe. Your name is too long, so I'm going to call you Nabe. I want you to be human."

He looked at me with eyes full of surprise and he blinked. "You know I'm a demon, don't you?"

"Yes, but what does it matter? Don't you have powers?"

"Do you underestimate my powers?" he laughed.

"Oh, no, I didn't mean it like that. I just thought there would be a way."

"I can use my human form, but why would you want this?"

"Because I want to see you more often."

He stood there, thinking for a moment. He pursed his lips, reaching out to touch my face before he stopped and let out a sigh. "I'll do it. Are you happy now?"

"Great! Thank you!" I said jumping up and down.

I saw him hiding a smile, as he bid me farewell and disappeared.

Maybe it was because my aunt forbade it, maybe it was my chest tightening at his every word or the throbbing in my heart. I didn't know. In any case, nothing could stop me from being with him now. I only wanted him and no-one else, even if my aunt didn't like the idea of us being together. How could

she understand my own feelings? From the first time
I saw him, I knew it was love I felt for him.

CHAPTER 6

The Taste of Sin

It took a few days for Sara to talk to me again. That's what she did every time she got mad at someone. Stubborn to a fault, as Uncle Peter had once said. Nevertheless, I didn't stop seeing Nabe.

Sara soon found out I was going out with him, but I didn't intend to admit the truth to her, no matter how many times she asked. Finn often tried to follow me, but I always found a way to avoid him. The thing is, I lived in a village. If someone was to see me with Nabe, when he was using his human form, our relationship would be known to all the villagers.

One day, I urged him to take me to a beautiful place. I saw him thinking for a while and then, he held my hand.

"Hold me tight," he advised me.

"I'm trying," I replied and held him even tighter.

He spread his huge, beautiful wings and flew with me in his arms. I screamed a bit at first, but then I mustered the courage to look down. Everything was of exquisite beauty. I could see every house in the village, even ours. I also saw the river. The view was breathtaking.

After a while, we arrived at a place that looked like nobody had set foot on for years. There were ruins of some old palace, but now, only stones were left as its remains. A crumbling fountain highlighted the overgrown courtyard.

"This place was once my home. I lived here for many years in my human form, until someone I considered a friend betrayed me by telling everyone I was an evil demon, that came to spread illness and poverty. The people of the village were furious and burned everything down. This is all that's left of it. Since then, I have decided never to step foot to the human world again." He stopped for a while and seemed skeptical. I looked at his forehead, where a wrinkle appeared between his brows. I held my breath. At last, he sighed and continued, allowing me to breathe once more, "That is, until I found you. Heather, demons can't love, but how else do you explain what I feel about you now?"

"What do you feel?"

Without answering, he pushed me down onto the wet grass. He impatiently took all my clothes off, until I was completely naked. Fortunately, that day it wasn't that cold outside, otherwise I would have frozen to death. He gently stroked my hair and let some strands of it land on my chest. He didn't say anything about that mark. It was as if he hadn't seen it. He kissed me with passion and started moving down to my chest, then my belly and below. I shivered at his every touch. He took off his clothes, except for his sleeveless shirt. I didn't have the strength to question him about the reason.

"It may hurt a little," he said.

"It doesn't matter, you can continue," I replied, panting.

Without hesitation, he went inside me. I let out a moan of both pain and pleasure. Who would have imagined that this feeling would be so beautiful? *Of course it would be sweet... the taste of sin.* With each move, I felt less and less pain, until the only thing I could feel was pleasure. I couldn't think of anything else. I could sense his sweat dripping on my body, making me jerk with each drop. We had become one. Human, and demon. One moment was all that was needed. Just one moment to sin. Which god would forgive me now?

I went back home keeping my head low. I didn't regret what I had done, but I knew my future was now unsure. My hair was soaked and tangled. I still had the smell of wet grass on me. Before I got inside, I shook a little bit of mud off of my dress.

I didn't turn to look at Sara, who was sitting in the living room along with Peter and I quickly went to the bathroom. I must have spent quite a long time in there. When I realized it, I hurried to my room, but Sara was already there, waiting for me.

"You can't get away that easily, Eri. What have you done, my child? What have you done?" she exclaimed, obviously worried.

"Sara… But, how?" I wondered, terrified.

"I'm the one who raised you. I might not be your mother, but I know what you're doing behind my back. Do you still not understand?"

All I could think of was that she had seen what a mess I was when I came back, but what was I supposed to tell her now? That I went out and I thought it would be a great idea to roll over in the mud?

"I slept with Nabe," I finally said.

I saw all color disappear from her face. Her hands were trembling.

"Oh, Eri, my child. Why?"

"Because I love him, Sara."

"You love a demon?"

"Human, demon… What does it matter?"

"You can't. No! I won't allow this madness."

Madness? Maybe she's right. I might be mad… Madly in love. "You can't stop me from loving him. You might know his archetype, but he's not who you think he is. He is kind and gentle, and he loves me. He has feelings, unlike *you*."

My words must have hurt her a lot, because I saw her eyes narrowing, but also gathering up a wave of tears, that never managed to escape.

"That's enough, little lady. I think you've said enough for the day."

"You don't understand!"

"I don't have to understand. Don't you ever go near that demon again. He is going to hurt you and deceive you, like —" She never finished that sentence and I never asked her about it either. "Come with me to the kitchen. I'll make some medicine for you. I don't want little demons flying around my house. What's done is done."

I followed her, without saying a word. She wanted to protect me and I had no reason not to let her to.

The medicine she gave me was bitter and I barely managed to drink it all. After another discussion on this issue, I felt sleepy and went to bed.

*

When I woke up, I changed clothes and went straight to school without eating breakfast. The sky was gorgeous that day. It was as if the moon had kissed the sun and then left him with a bitter goodbye. On the way to school, I could see various demons everywhere, glancing at me threateningly. They must have been lesser demons, not as powerful as Nabe. It was the first time I saw their kind in the world of the living and that terrified me.

I also learned why all these creatures could never enter my house; Nabe had put some kind of spell around it. At least I knew I was safe inside. Whatever happened, I could just lock myself in.

"Good morning," Christie said. "Heather!" she repeated when I didn't answer her the first time and moved her hands back and forth to catch my attention.

I jolted. "Christie! I'm sorry. I got absorbed in my thoughts."

"I figured that out. Do you want to tell me why you are like this?"

"Like what?"

She put both her hands on her hips. "I don't know, you tell me."

"Come on. This isn't the right time to be talking about this," I looked around, wanting to disappear.

"Did something happen between you and Finn?"

"No, it has nothing to do with him," I said a bit abruptly.

"Then, what happened? I can't bear to see you like that."

"I, uhm… I slept with someone," I said blushing.

Her eyes widened. "You did what?" she shouted with surprise.

"Quiet! I don't want the rest of the village to know."

"Who was it?"

"I can't tell you that yet, Christie."

She looked at me sneakily. "And? Do you regret it?"

"No."

I didn't really regret it. I felt weird after Sara's scolding and I started doubting him and his love for me. I knew he loved me, but her words were seeping in me like poison.

"Did you like it?"

My body could still remember his touch. "Very much."

"Oh, Heather. Now you made me jealous. I wish I also had a lover."

"You'll find someone, one day, I'm sure of it."

"Do you think that someone could be Finn?"

"Christie!"

We both burst out laughing.

We've been chatting with Christie for a long time about many things and also continued our conversation after we finished our classes. So, I came home late and Sara started questioning me.

"Why are you so late? Who were you with? What were you doing for so long?"

"Sara… I was just talking to Christie and I got distracted. You don't have to ask me the same questions every time."

"Fine. Let's eat now. I just served dinner."

We all sat together at the table as a family and ate. I still had the bitter taste of my aunt's medicine in my mouth and I couldn't tell if the food was delicious or not. When I finished eating, I went to my room. I wanted to call Nabe so much, but I didn't know what to say. I was very confused, but I felt that something tied us together, as if it was meant for me to meet him. I was always taught not to mess with fate, because what was meant to happen, would, and there was no way to prevent that.

CHAPTER 7

The Truth

My body was always craving for Nabe. I wanted to be with him; with a demon, for all I cared. My aunt was right, but that didn't mean I should listen to her. I kept seeing him in secret. It never lasted long, only a few minutes. All I wanted was to see him smiling at me, caring for me, being with me… Nothing else really mattered.

Sara gradually stopped questioning me about where I was and who I was with. She had an exceptional intuition and, deep inside, I believe she knew I was still seeing Nabe. Her eyes kept silently studying my expressions and my every move, but I ignored her. I tried my best to keep my secret hidden.

What was so wrong with being in love with a demon? He wasn't like the others.

The creatures and demons around me were still gazing at me wherever I went. One day, one of them pushed me and I fell down. Until then, I had no idea they could touch me. Seemed like I was wrong. It scared the hell out of me. Why would they attack me all of a sudden?

"Nabe," I whispered and he immediately appeared by my bedroom's window.

"You asked for me?"

"There's something extremely strange about all these creatures that are lingering around me. They never tried to harm me before, but now they seem really hostile towards me – especially the demons. I'm scared."

He frowned upon my words. "They are waiting… to see if you are pregnant from me."

I looked at him astonished. "Why?" That was the only thing I managed to ask, while also trying to keep my voice as quiet as possible.

"If you are, they are going to kill you. They believe a child born from human and demon is a bad omen with impure blood."

Sara knocked on my door and when I turned my gaze to the window again, Nabe had already disappeared. My heart was beating fast and I was still shocked from his revelation. I opened the door to my aunt. She only wanted to check on me. Would I never be able to hide from her?

*

It was now spring and my school years were finally coming to an end. Christie and I decided to go horse riding to the city, because she wanted to buy a new dress. The weather was nice and the sun shone upon us. The city wasn't very far from our little village. There were all kinds of shops; one could buy dresses, hats, shoes, flowers and different kinds of jewelry. There were also a bakery and a breathtaking toy shop.

"Heather, how does this dress look?"

"Don't you think it's a bit too revealing?"

"Not for me! Come on, let's go in and see what else they've got."

We finally went in and looked at the carefully sewn dresses. They were very expensive. I didn't see anything that could completely cover my chest. I couldn't wear such a dress, because of my birthmark. Christie, on the other hand, was in love with that kind of dresses.

At that moment, I turned my gaze to the shop window. I saw a familiar figure staring at me and felt my heart race. Without being able to control my body, I walked mechanically to his side. My eyes revealed my excitement and he understood immediately. He looked at me, his gaze showing how much he had missed me. *He used his human form this time.*

"You haven't called for me these days," he finally said.

"Sara became suspicious of me again and I could never find the right moment to call you. Why did you come now?"

"I couldn't wait any longer. I've told you before; I don't have the strength to stay away from you."

"Oh, Nabe… I am so sorry. I really wanted to see you, too. When you are not with me, I feel as if I'm not truly living."

I saw him smile, relieved, and I smiled back at him. Then, Christie came out of the shop, holding a box in her hands, and interrupted us, "Heather! I found a dress! Where have you –?"

"Christie! Uhm, this is my friend, Nabe."

"Nice to meet you," she said somewhat awkwardly and held the box tighter in her hands.

"Likewise," he replied.

We sat on a bench for a while, a bit further away from the shop, and we talked. As if he somehow knew, Finn came out of nowhere, riding on his horse. As soon as he saw me with Nabe, I saw his relaxed smile disappear. I greeted him, of course, like nothing happened. I introduced him to Nabe, and as I was already feeling uncomfortable, I made a gesture to Christie telling her to leave with Finn. She wouldn't want to miss that chance.

"You won't let me go back alone, will you?" she said, and looked at me with a sneaky expression.

He seemed surprised, but he did not deny, even though his face was full of disappointment. Eventually, they left, each on their horse, and followed the road back to the village.

We were left alone now. The city was extremely quiet that day. The sun was shining brightly upon our heads, so bright that I had to cover my eyes with my hand. The smell of fresh bread being baked filled up my nose. Nabe could smell it, too. He seemed to enjoy the peace and quiet. For a moment, he closed his eyes, probably forgetting I was with him.

"You know, I'm here, too," I pouted and crossed my arms. He jolted and opened his eyes. I giggled. *A demon jolted?* I could as well die laughing at that moment. "I knew you were not paying attention. Where is your mind traveling to?"

I blushed as he stared at my green eyes and slowly leaned closer to my face. He pressed his lips against mine, in a passionate kiss that took my breath away. He caressed my hair tenderly, as if we hadn't seen each other for ages. When I opened my eyes, I saw a demon rushing toward us threateningly. It seemed Nabe was too distracted to sense his own kind.

"Behind you!" I shouted and felt an icy shiver down my spine.

Without wasting any time, he changed back to his normal form, becoming invisible to the human eye on his will, and black flames rose around him. He immediately attacked the demon, forcing him to take a step back. His enemy didn't seem ready to give up yet. I was his target and that made it hard for Nabe to fight. While he was protecting me, I began to wonder for how long those demons would keep threatening me. If I were to bear the child of a demon, they wouldn't let me live. I knew that very well and I was glad I wasn't pregnant. I would have known by then.

Suddenly, I saw that demon tear Nabe's shirt with a small dagger. He fell on his knees and thick drops of blood began to drip unto the ground.

"Nabe!"

He didn't answer. He rose up like a furious beast and killed the demon with one powerful hit, showing no mercy to the heartless creature.

When he turned to me, I didn't look at his smile, nor his wound. I saw that mark; the heather. That damned mark I had since the day I was born. I wasn't looking at my own chest, but his. Now, my expression was full of distrust and fear. And he understood it immediately. His wound closed, but the mark was still there. He tried to explain, but I had already taken my horse and moved, as quickly as I could, towards my house.

When I arrived, Sara was waiting for me with a plate full of food on the table. She seemed worried, when she saw me like that.

"What happened, my child? Did you see a ghost?"

"No, Sara." Irritated, I tore my dress and showed her the mark.

She was confused. "What are you trying to tell me with this?"

"This is what I saw."

"You've had this since you were young."

"Not on me, Sara."

Suddenly, Nabe appeared in his human form, his shirt still torn. "Heather, at least let me explain."

"Here, I saw it on him."

"Naberius! Is that how you, demons, keep your promises and secrets?"

"Trust me, I didn't know this was going to happen!"

"I don't know what to believe anymore!"

Without fully understanding what was going on and why both of them were talking like they knew each other, I hit the table with my hand, so loud that Peter and Finn ran to see what was happening.

"Is everything all right here?" asked Uncle Peter.

"You!" Finn said, looking suspiciously at Nabe.

"Peter, Finn, this is not the right moment. Go away. We'll talk later." My aunt pointed out to them and they obeyed without saying another word. Her gaze must have been absolutely terrifying for them to leave that easily.

"Can you at least explain to me exactly what's happening? Like it or not, I'm not that stupid. I know that, in order for my mark to be on the body of a demon, it means that I have signed some sort of contract with him. Throughout my whole life, I don't remember doing this, unless the demons can get in touch with the babies, too!" I screamed, totally annoyed.

"Eri… When you were born, your heart was weak and wasn't able to keep you alive. Your mother, in a moment of despair, called Naberius. In exchange for her life, he would save yours, until his powers run out," she said as calmly as she could.

"Until when? When were you planning to tell me? When it would be too late? Nabe? Do you have anything to say about all this? What am I to you? Another baby you saved? Do I owe you a favor now?"

"Heather, listen to me, I'm begging you. I've never made a deal with a human for their life or someone else's before. All contracts were usually for money, love, revenge… but never like yours. When I heard your mother's words, I immediately showed up without thinking, as if I couldn't control myself. From the moment I saw you, I felt like I had to save you somehow. The only way I knew back then, was to take a human's life, for me to be able to have enough strength to share my heart with yours. Your mother offered her own life, and yours will end when I no longer have any more strength to share with you."

"You killed my mother just to kill me, too, in the end? But, of course; you're a demon. What else could I expect of you?"

"Heather, wait!"

I grabbed a light coat to cover my chest and left running from my house, heading to the river. I thought I could calm down there, but Nabe came after me.

"Go away! I have nothing else to say to you," I said bluntly and wiped a teardrop that escaped from my eyes.

"Don't talk then, just listen."

I made a gesture for him to continue.

"Heather, forgive me, please. If you wish never to see me again, I'll do it. I'll stay away from you, though I know that this isn't what you want. So, tell me, is there anything I can do to earn your forgiveness?"

How much longer should I let him beg me? How unusual; a demon to apologize. Finally, I turned my gaze at him. "Do you want me to forgive you?" I asked.

"Of course."

"Then leave and come back only when you find the most beautiful thing on this earth and bring it with you."

He bowed, as if I was his master and disappeared immediately.

I waited for a long time that I started to feel drowsy. The anger inside me had already started to wear off. In a flash, Nabe was back. He was… smiling at me. So carefree and blissful. A few moments ago, I was mad at him and ordered him around and now he came back smiling? He kept looking at me like he just realized how much he loved me.

"You came back empty-handed and you're smiling like a small child. Is that how much you want me to forgive you? Are you mocking me?

"I didn't bring anything for you, because I couldn't find what you were looking for."

"You could bring me a flower, a jewel… There are many beautiful things in the world."

"You asked for the most beautiful one. And that, my dear, is right in front of me. No matter how much I search, I'll never encounter anything as beautiful as you."

My heart skipped a beat and my eyes filled up with happy tears. Upon hearing those words, I knew I had already forgiven him. He didn't waste any time. He kissed me with all the passion that only somebody who loves deeply can kiss, and embraced me, before leaving once again.

When I returned home, I took off my coat and went to the living room. Sara was waiting for me, while reading a book.

"Eri, you're back! Is everything all right?"

"As good as it can be, when you know you're going to die soon, and the clock has already been ticking from the day you were born."

Sara's gaze clouded and she let out a sigh. "Don't think about it, my child. Try to make the most out of the time you have left."

*

As days went by, I realized that, even if I had more time, I wouldn't be able to do all the things I wanted to. I often called Nabe and spent many hours together with him. Most of the time, we were riding on our horses, or sitting by the river. I loved that place. We even went to the waterfall, which was located just outside the village. That place was ethereal, although no-one visited it because it was inaccessible.

"Nabe… When I die, I want you to promise me something."

"What is it?"

"You will never make another contract like this with a human. My mother could have just let me die. She would still be alive with another child, one who would be healthy and live for many years. What is the point of all this now?"

"I won't do it again, I promise. Your mother just wanted you to live a little longer."

"I know, but I'd prefer things to be different."

He embraced me.

*

The school ended and along with it, ended the summer. Autumn came and trees lost their first leaves. I adored the sound they made when I stepped on them, the crunching, crinkling. It used to rain a lot in that season and the sky was pretty much always dull.

I found out that Christie and Finn were now together and they were even planning to get married. That was something I never expected to happen, but I was tremendously delighted for both of them. He found his destined partner and Christie got the man of her dreams.

CHAPTER 8

Ashes

Days kept passing me by and Nabe started visiting me less and less, until he stopped answering my calls. I was so worried, but he once told me that if something were to happen to him, the mark would disappear. For now, it was still on my chest.

One of those autumn days, an unknown demon suddenly appeared in my room and I jolted from my fear. *How did he enter? Our house is protected by Nabe's powers!*

"Who are you?" I asked timidly.

"I'm Phoenix. Don't be afraid, Naberius sent me here. He is very weak, so he can no longer come to the world of the living."

So, that's why…

"What's going to happen now?" I exclaimed worried.

"You have to come with me."

"Wait. I have to say goodbye to my family."

I got out of the room and run down the stairs.

"Sara, I need to go. It's time to say goodbye."

"Eri… So soon?"

"I have to hurry. Nabe's power is running out. Thank you for raising me like your own child. I love you. All of you."

Sara could hardly stand on her feet. "Is there no other way?"

"I wish there was."

"Please, my dearest child, can't you just stay forever?"

"It's already hard for me to leave you. Don't make it harder, I beg of you," I said with a pained expression on my face.

She embraced me, tears flowing from her eyes and she kissed me on the forehead. When their turn came, Peter and Finn bid me farewell with a hug and some held-back tears. Sara made sure to explain the situation to them after I found out the truth.

"Follow me," the demon said and opened a gate.

We went in and found ourselves in a dark corridor. There was fog everywhere and it was difficult to see in front of us. I felt like we had been walking for ages. Eventually, we arrived in front of a huge gate. The demon approached first and opened the doors with some odd words.

"Whatever you see, remember that you are in the world of the dead now."

I shivered to the sound of that word.

A huge monster with three heads stood in front of me. He was looking at the gate and waited impatiently to see who would pass by. He stood aside when he saw Phoenix, but he stared at me furiously.

Beyond the huge doors, I saw hot lava flowing everywhere and souls burning in restless flames; their wailing piercing my ears. The temperature felt like it was burning my skin, but not a single drop of sweat streamed down my face. I saw demons fighting against each other and practicing their powers. Some looked at me strangely and others threateningly.

"Listen, Naberius asked for a favor before I bring you to him. Come with me. This way."

I followed him without speaking. He seemed nervous and I thought that maybe we shouldn't be there.

"Inside this room are the souls of those who have called demons and signed contracts with them. I will wait for you here. Don't stay there for too long."

The door creaked when I opened it. Inside there were cells, where souls were imprisoned. There were young and elderly people. There were children, too. I understood why I was there. I didn't know my mother's face, so I glanced briefly at the cells and moved on. Some people were shouting at me, begging me to release them, but I ignored them and continued my search.

"Here! Behind you!" I heard a voice whisper, and saw one of the souls making a gesture through the prison bars, for me to go closer. I approached and observed her face. I didn't look like her, after all.

"Mother?" I asked and saw her bursting into tears.

She reached out her almost transparent hand, out of the cell's bars, and gently touched my cheek. It felt like a gentle warm breeze was caressing me. "My dearest child, I'm so glad to see you, even if it's just for a while. The time has come, hasn't it?"

"I never thought I would ever see you in this life. I came to return the heart to the demon."

"You cannot imagine how much I regret that I sealed your own fate. Back then, I wanted a better life for you, but it turned out I was only thinking of my own life. Now it's too late. Could you ever forgive me?"

"Don't worry, mother. I have already forgiven you. I'm grateful for all the years I was able to live."

She smiled tenderly at me. "Let me tell you something before you leave. Naberius is not an evil demon. When he accompanied my soul here, he told me that he would do everything for you to live as many years as possible, and that he would take care of you for the rest of your short life."

"And he did. Mother, I don't need any more time, really. I'm so happy I got to see you. Goodbye, for now."

"Farewell, my child."

I left my mother and returned to where Phoenix was waiting. I hardly managed to hold back the tears that filled my eyes. There was no feeling strong enough to describe the pain I felt, now that I had to say goodbye to my mother once again.

"They'll punish me if they find out I brought you here. Let's go. We don't have much time left."

I silently followed him as we climbed the endless, half-ruined stairs. A little further, I saw Nabe on his knees, weak.

"Nabe!" I cried out his name and ran to his side.

"Heather… I'm sorry I couldn't come. My powers have almost run out. I thought I could survive a little longer, but I'm afraid this is it. You see, when we, demons, share one of our organs, our powers obtain an expiration date, which depends on how powerful we already are. I might have been able to last a little longer, if I hadn't used my human form as much as I did. Although it doesn't really matter anymore."

"I came to return what's yours," I said determined.

"Look at me. I've lived for ages in this world and I grew tired of it. I can't live another eternity without you. Take this and put it on your mark. It is the rest of the heart you need to survive."

He gave me a black crystal with a bizarre shape that looked like a heart. I immediately understood what it meant, and tears flowed from my eyes. "No, please! I can't live without you either. I can't do this!"

"Heather, I'm begging you. There's no more time. Set me free."

"I love you, Nabe. I don't want to lose you."

"I love you, too. If fate is on our side, we'll meet again. Perhaps in another life… Who knows? So, please, do it and don't hesitate anymore."

With shaking hands, I put the crystal on my chest and it disappeared along with that mark. Nabe started fading into a cloud of burning ashes, slowly and torturing, as was appropriate for a demon. In the end, he disappeared with a painful smile on his face and a teardrop that stabbed my heart like a sharp knife. He left behind a black feather, which I held tightly in my hands.

I stayed there for a while, sobbing, screaming, embracing the void… I was all alone now, without the one I loved more than anything in this world.

When I managed to calm down, I stood on my feet and decided to go back. Arriving at the enormous gate, I kept trying, in vain, to open it. Without the mark I could no longer see the demons and there was no-one there to help me.

Before I had time to panic, a black shadow appeared out of nowhere, making me shiver. He stood imposingly in front of me. "You want to leave, but only I, the King of Hell, can open these gates for you. I know why you are here. I have reigned for ages and not once did a demon fail me. Naberius has always been softer than the others, but I never expected that he would prefer to save a human over himself. You must be special, so I will ask you a question. If you answer correctly, only then will I let you go."

I took a deep breath. "I'm all ears."

"If you could choose between a short life and eternity, which one would be your choice?"

"A short life. What good is an eternity to me, if I can't be with the ones I love?"

He let out a loud scoff. "You will find new people to love. If you stay by my side, I will give you everything you ever wanted."

"You have no idea what I want," I raised my voice.

"Is that so?" he said scornfully, his eyes narrowing into a thin line.

The gates in front of me were never opened. Instead, the ground below crumbled and sucked me inside. I kept falling, sinking deeper and deeper into the darkness. I landed somewhere that felt like sand. Even if I had my eyes open, there was no light. Everything was black.

"Find your way out and I will let you return to your short life. Fail, and you will be trapped here forever," his voice echoed.

How am I supposed to get out of here, when I can't even see? I was getting worried. What if I didn't make it? Was there a time limit? Suddenly I was being played with by Hell's King. A game, where the chances of me coming back alive were very slim. "Great..." I murmured.

It was like I was in a place where all life has disappeared from the earth. I didn't feel hot or cold. I didn't even know if there was any oxygen. I couldn't feel any trace of wind, nor could I smell anything. It was the absolute nothingness.

Somewhere further away from me, I heard Nabe's familiar voice. *Could it be?* I blindly tried to follow it, leading me to an exquisite scenery, dimly lit, inside that darkness. A colorful meadow, where a family played freely, laughing and dancing to nature's sounds. Nabe, our child and I. What a nostalgic sight... It brought tears to my eyes. Then, I noticed a door behind them.

Instinctively, I turned my head behind. There was another scenery, along with another door. My mother and my father were there, both perfectly alive. They were sitting on a sofa, singing a lullaby to a small child... me. They seemed genuinely happy together. I took a few steps closer and reached out for the door. *My parents, huh?* I wasn't able to feel their warmth and they never sang lullabies for me... *If I choose this door, it will certainly lead me to them.*

And then, it hit me; my parents weren't alive. There was absolutely no chance they would come back to life, so I would probably end up dead and trapped in Hell for all eternity. Another poor soul to be thrown into the fire.

I run towards the other door, as fast as I could and reached for the knob. Without looking back, I entered. A dazzling light blinded my eyes for a moment. When I was able to open them again, I realized I was outside Hell's gates.

"His soul is no longer here. If you want to look for him, look up when you return to your world. Surely, the angels will take him in their arms," the voice said.

*

Back home, everyone was delighted that I was alive. Sara prepared my favorite food and also made a cake, but I couldn't taste the flavors, and nothing seemed to please me anymore. I looked at the feather in my hand and teared up. *The years I have left will pass by slowly from now on.*

EPILOGUE

A friend told me this story once, and now it's time for me to tell it to you.

When Nabe died, his soul was transferred to heaven. There, it would be weighed, so that it could be decided whether he'd return to Hell, or he'd stay in heaven.

An angel appeared in front of him. He had six wings, two of which covered his face, two covered his legs, and the other two were probably used for flying. "Naberius."

"Azrael. I'm glad to see you again."

"Me, too. I see that you did what I told you to. No demon had ever stepped foot here. No-one, but you. And you begged to save a human's life instead of yours. I see the crystal I gave you went to the right hands. You never were like the other demons. You didn't want power or glory; all you wanted was to help people, in any way you could."

"Maybe it's because I wanted to be like them. I never liked eternity."

"I can't turn you back into a demon. Though I can give you another chance to live, as an angel this time, because you chose to give your life to save a human."

"Azrael, you know very well that I don't want to stay here. Do me a favor and send my soul to Hell. Let me burn there."

"Did you love that girl so much?"

"I think I proved it. I let her live."

"Listen to me, Naberius. Since you don't wish to become one of us, I will send you to the world of the living as a human being."

"Will you actually do that?"

The angel was skeptical for a while. Eventually, he opened a white door and ordered him to go through.

And he became a human, just as the angel promised. He came back to the world of the living, looking for the only person he loved more than his own life. And there, he found me; at the river's bank, I was gazing at the water that was flowing endlessly, moving on, and leaving the past behind.

When he approached me, I looked at him with eyes full of surprise and disbelief. He opened his hand

and showed me a black feather. Tears of happiness escaped from my eyes and I jumped in his arms.

Now, we were both humans. Nothing and no-one could separate us anymore. So many dreams were waiting to become reality. We had an entire life ahead of us.

Author Bio

Despoina Kemeridou was born in 1996 in Thessaloniki, Greece. She studied Midwifery at the International University of Greece.

She has been into landscape photography since 2017. In her free time, she likes to draw. She started writing in 2009 and hence, understood that this is what she always wanted to do.

Her first book, Fated to Meet You, was self-published in 2018. She self-published her second book, Mark of a Demon, in 2020. Currently, she's working on her upcoming dark poetry collection called "Of Darkness and Light".

Fated to meet You

"I love you with every fiber of my being, Eleanor, but this love won't keep me alive, nor will it be able to protect you."

When Nora finds herself in the past, away from her mundane life, she chooses to take the place of a dead Princess. An arranged marriage with the soon-to-be King of the neighboring kingdom will help her discover love, friendship and hidden secrets.

An ancient curse has been haunting the royal family for ages. Will she be able to break it and save her loved ones from the cruel hands of death?

Time is already running out...